Judy Schachner

Sarabella's Thinking Cap

Dial Books for Young Readers

For WES librarian Martha Lambertsen, teacher Dan Fantozzi,
and his class of terrific third-grade thinkers.

Extra love to my own Sarabella.

Dial Books for Young Readers
Penguin Young Readers Group
An imprint of Penguin Random House LLC
375 Hudson Street
New York, NY 10014

CIP Data is available

Printed in China
ISBN 9780525429180

10 9 8 7 6 5 4 3

Design by Lily Malcom
Text set in Sabon MT Std

The art for this book was created in acrylics,
gouache, collage, and mixed media.

Sarabella had no time for small talk.
In fact, she never talked much at all…
because she was too busy thinking.

She thought about big things

and small things…

and oodles of in-between things,
like ants and uncles and doodles of poodles.

Pinky's thoughts would remain
a mystery, but there was nothing
mysterious about her family.

They loved puppets,

painting pictures,

and playing guitar.

Most of all they loved their
Sarabella just the way she was,
with her feet on the ground
and her head in the clouds.

To Sarabella there was nowhere she would rather be than dreaming of painted ponies racing across the sky.

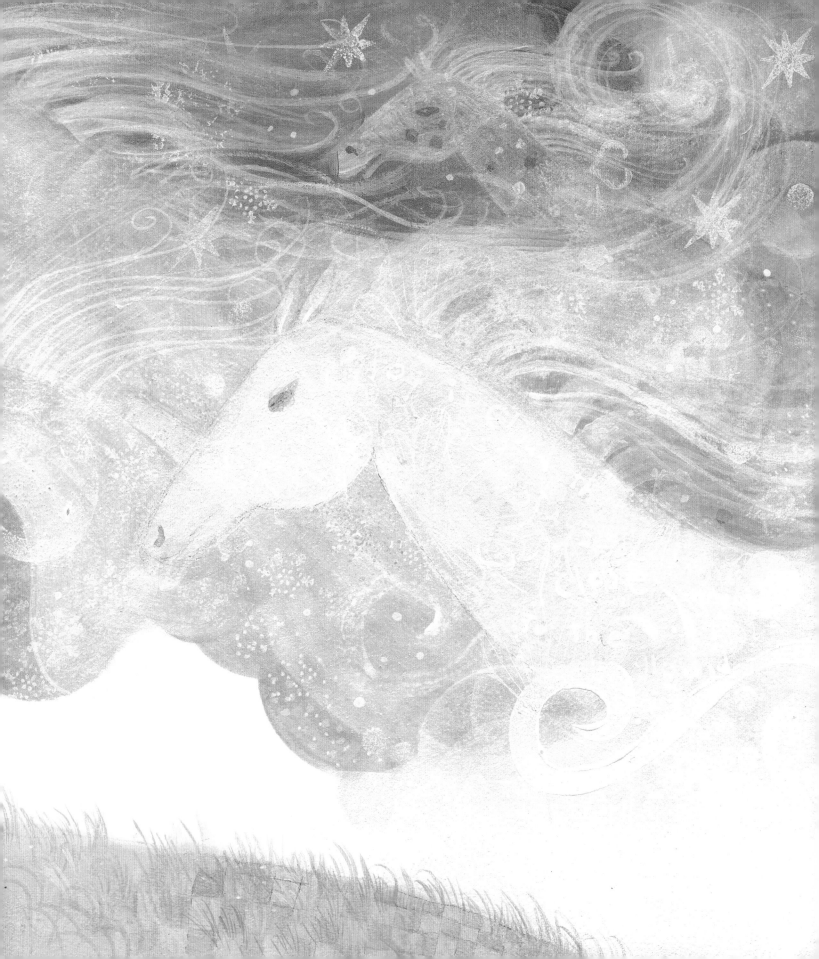

Some ideas came as a complete surprise to her, while other notions were coddled and cared for like rare plants in a well-loved garden.

"I need to read up on you, Mister."

a black mustache

a pair of pants

Ponder Question Mull
hammer out
Reflect Wonder
consider
Study Reason Stew Estimate
imagine Meditate Weigh Ruminate
bear in mind

rice pudding

There was never a doubt that
Sarabella had a green thumb for thinking.
The problem was—no one ever knew
what she was thinking *about*.

Her teacher, Mr. Fantozzi, had a knack for knowing just what Sarabella *wasn't* thinking about. And that was schoolwork. Sometimes all it took was a word, a sound, or the scent of Samantha's Magic Markers to carry her thoughts away.

Sarabella needs to find a way.
To focus and finish her work
on time.

A B C

Mr. Fantozzi

Sarabella needs to find a way
to share her thoughts. We are
all very curious and it might
help her concentrate on her work.
Mr. Fantozzi

Sarabella ... to spend more time
thinking about schoolwork
and less time thinking about
unicorns, kittens, and clouds.
Not that there is anything wrong
with those things.
Mr. Fantozzi

Sarabella is well behaved
and thoughtful, but her head is
in the clouds. She needs a
pair of heavy shoes.

Dear Parents,
Sarabella disappeared
today. Must learn to
focus.
Mr. Fantozzi

We'd all love to know
what Sarabella thinks
about. Mr. Fantozzi

I'd love to know where
Sarabella goes when
she's sitting at her desk.
Z G B
Mr. Fantozzi

And that's when Mr. F, who was really very
nice, had to send her home with another note.
And this made Sarabella feel terrible.

The notes never upset her parents because
once upon a time they got sent home
with notes, too.
"Really?" said Sarabella.
"Really," replied her mom. "You have
daydreams in your DNA."

At bedtime Sarabella cuddled up to her big sister, Cece. "I wish I knew how to focus," said Sarabella.

"It's easy," said Cece. "All you have to do is take deep breaths and squint."

At school the next day, Sarabella followed her sister's advice, but all she got was a dizzy spell and a visit to the school nurse for an eye test.

One night, during a math facts-memorizing meltdown,
a bear of a thought dropped by for a chat.
"I have a good head for numbers," he said.
"I can see that," replied Sarabella.
"Keep me in mind if you ever
   need help," said the bear.
"I'll consider it," said Sarabella.
   And that was her first mistake.

The second was taking the bear to school the next day.
"I sure hope you left some room in your head for math facts," said her sister.

There was always room in Sarabella's brain for one more tantalizing thought...

Just not math facts.

By the time they arrived in class, the bear had fallen asleep, but waiting in the wings was an odd flock of birds who didn't know the difference between an egg and the number 8.

That's when she heard Mr. F calling out her nickname.
"Earth to Cerebellum," he said. "A penny for
your thoughts."
"She's not thinking," said Russell. "She's daydreaming."
"Daydreaming is an awesome kind of thinking,"
said Mr. F. "But not during class."

That afternoon Sarabella stayed in at recess to catch up on her work. She liked sitting at the round table in the quiet room.

"I know you can do this, Sarabella," said Mr. F, handing her the very last quiz. "Just put on your thinking cap and focus."

Sarabella began to imagine what her thinking cap might look like. And then she turned back to her papers.

Right before the bell rang, Mr. F had
Sarabella hand out the weekend assignment.
They were always something fun.

"What do you think, Sarabella?"
asked Mr. F.
An otter popped into her mind.
But that was just the first thing.

A Penny for Your Thoughts
Draw a picture of your favorite daydreams.

A Penny for Your Thoughts
Draw a picture of your favorite daydreams.

Before she even got home, kissed Pinky, and put on her comfy bunny slippers, Sarabella had already thought of a thousand extraordinary things.

By dinnertime she'd run out of
paper, had an upset tummy and
a great big mess on her hands.

That night just as Sarabella was about to give up, a whale of a thought appeared on the horizon. The closer it got, the more beautiful it became.

And though it was the most enormous creature
she had ever seen, Sarabella felt unafraid.

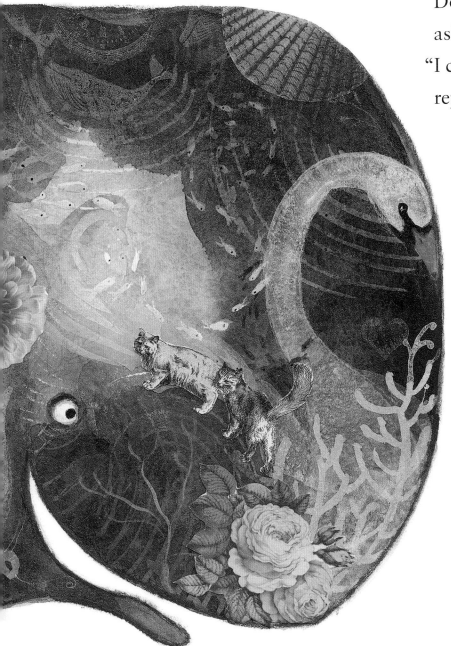

"Do you know what I think?"
asked the whale.
"I can see what you think,"
replied Sarabella.
"And so should everyone else,"
said the whale.
**"To *share it, you've
just got to wear it.*"**

Then the whale blew Sarabella
a kiss before she swam off.

This gave Sarabella an idea. She found a
brown paper bag and a ruler for measuring.
Then she rounded up some old magazines,
pretty papers, pencils, pastels,
stickers, and stamps, along
with her favorite drawings.

For the rest of the night she clipped
and colored, pasted and painted,
until her project was done.

Monday morning everyone was
eager to share their weekend project.
"A penny for your thoughts," said Mr. F
as the kids sat crisscross applesauce on the floor.
"Who's going first?"

To the surprise of all, it was Sarabella.
"*If you want to share it,*" she said,
standing up in front of the class,
"*you've just got to wear it.*"

a set of false teeth

a cross-eyed potato

And that's exactly what Sarabella did
when she placed the most spectacular
collection of doodles and daydreams
right on top of her head.

a Town called
Saint Cloud

eye I

a laughing donkey

Like School

"So that's what you've been thinking!" said the kids in awe.
Lara saw unicorns, and Xavi saw planets. Dylan saw a cat,
a snake, and a feather, while Nate reported seeing clouds
with a touch of bad weather.

"A penny for *your* thoughts, Mr. F," said Sarabella.

"I think," he said with a smile, "your thoughts are worth
more than all the pennies in the world."

A penny for your thoughts
My brain is exciting

A penny for your thoughts

A penny for your thoughts

On Tuesday Bob came to school wearing a thinking cap of his own.
Sarabella really liked it. "We have a lot in common," said Bob.
"My thoughts exactly," agreed Sarabella.